THE CRUISE
OF THE
AARDVARK

THE CRUISE OF THE AARDVARK

by OGDEN NASH

pictures by Wendy Watson

M. EVANS AND COMPANY   NEW YORK

Library of Congress Catalog Card Number 67-27296

M. Evans and Company, Inc.
216 East 49 Street
New York, New York 10017

Printed in the United States of America

9 8 7 6 5 4 3 2 1

The aardvark is a useful beast;
On ants and termites doth he feast.
One day, because of what he ate,
His teeth grew TU-BU-LI-DEN-TATE,

Which means, both top and underneath,
They look like tubes instead of teeth,
And prove to be, by happy chance,
Exactly right for chewing ants.
Then, though the word may make you smile,
His sticky tongue is EX-TEN-SILE.
That means that he can thrust it out
For yards and yards beyond his snout,
The very thing for trapping, say,
A termite half a mile away.

I know one aardvark so remarkable
His story might be called aard-varkable.
It's strange but true, and what is more,
It never has been told before.

Aardvark awoke one rainy morn
And wished he never had been born.
The earth in soggy darkness lay,
The sky was like a bowl of gray,
A bowl some giant hand was tipping;
Everything in the world was dripping.

The lowlands dripped,
The highlands dripped,
The continents and islands dripped,
The bushes dripped,
The mosses dripped,
And Aardvark's own proboscis dripped.
Yes, even Aardvark's nose was runny
On a day the weatherman promised Sunny.

Aardvark's breast was dull with gloom;
Glumly he crawled across the room,
But you should have seen his glumness pass
When he gazed into the looking-glass.

"O Aardvark, Aardvark," chanted he,
"How happy am I that thou art me.
Thou leadest all creatures alphabetically,
Also in beauty, which means AES-THET-I-CAL-LY.
Aardvark, thou art a joy forever,
A creature modest, brave, and clever.
Thy teeth, thou TU-BU-LI-DEN-TATE mammal,
They have no roots and no enamel;
Thy ears like mule's, thy snorkel snout
Cause envious animals to pout,
While ants and termites teach their young
To flee thy sticky EX-TEN-SILE tongue;
But when thou art prepared to sup,
Thy raking claws will dig them up.
Who called the lion king of beasts?
It is on thee my eyesight feasts!
O Aardvark, what a lucky earth
That it was chosen for thy birth!
And what a glorious earth 'twould be
If everyone resembled thee!"

Now Aardvark clapped his claws in bliss
And blew the mirror a farewell kiss.
He watched the rain fall drop by drop
Which even an aardvark couldn't stop;
So much more rain than he could use
He thought he'd take a tropical cruise.
(A tropical cruise, I might explain,
Takes people away from mud and rain.
They climb aboard a handsome boat
And off on sunny seas they float.
Through sunny tropic isles they roam
Until the sun comes out at home.)

He packed his sketchbook and his pencils,
His paints and brushes and art utensils,
Because he was, as you should know,
An aardvark Michelangelo.
Then, singing "Toodle-oo, pip-pip!"
He sallied forth to seek his ship.

His ship he sought, his ship he found,
Half in the water and half aground.
Aardvark uttered a cry of joy;
To be exact, 'twas "Ship ahoy!"
A monkey lowered a slippery plank
To where he stood on slippery bank.
He scrambled aboard, and just in time,
For a raging flood began to climb,
And aided by the extra flooding
The ship across the waves went scudding.

Said Aardvark, drawing himself erect,
"You know who *I* am, I expect.
I'm sure you never thought to see
A shipmate eminent as me,
I'm sure you feel inclined to stammer,
To watch your p's and q's and grammar;
I'm sure that you would much prefer

To make a bow and call me Sir.
But let me state in terms emphatic,
I'm really very democratic.
In fact I'm ready, in a word,
To mingle with the common herd.
To share your simple life I'm happy.
Now take my luggage, and make it snappy!"

The animals gawked, as at one daft,
Then coarsely the hyena laughed.
"Our simple life is rough and rugged;
If your lordship wants your luggage lugged
Down in the hold to your quarters snug
I suggest that you pick it up and lug."
"Just step this way," said a platypus maiden,
And Aardvark followed, luggage-laden,
To a cabin the size of a medicine cabinet
With scarcely room to swing a crab in it.

It seemed more like a prison cell,
But Aardvark smiled and said, "Oh well,
I'll learn to love this cozy nook;
Now, if you please, send up the cook.

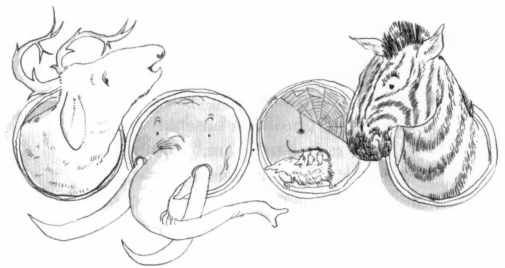

Don't stand there gaping! Are you deaf?
I said, send up the cook, the chef!"

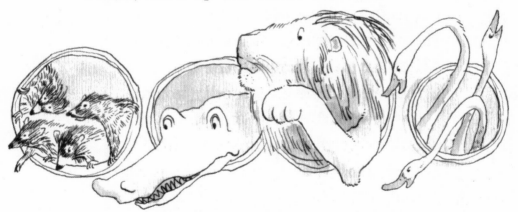

A wapiti smiled, a wallaby tittered,
A dingo sneered, a flamingo twittered.
Aardvark ignored the whole caboodle

Till up there strutted an elegant poodle,
With snowy apron and tall white hat
And a rolling pin like a baseball bat.
"Bon jour, monsieur! I am," said he,
"Ze greatest chef zere ever be,
And once my omelette you have taste,
You gain nine inches round ze waist."
Said Aardvark, "Chef, be at your ease,
My palate is not hard to please.
The plainest sort of fare is mine:
On ants I breakfast, lunch, and dine.
Prepare them any way you wish;
I'll guarantee to clean the dish.
I'm sure you have a goodly hoard,
I saw two as I came aboard,
So pleasing plump, so shiny black;
Pray bring them to me for a snack."
The poodle chef began to cough
So hard his hat came toppling off.
"I cook ze turnip, cook ze carrot,
Ze sunflower seed like for ze parrot,

Ze soufflé like we cook in France,
But nevaire can I cook ze ants!"
"You cannibal!" cried the platypus,
"The ants are passengers, just like us!"

"Begone," said Aardvark, "vamoose, get hence;
The captain shall hear of your insolence!"
The animals gave a loud horse laugh,
And Aardvark was told by a rude giraffe,
"The captain is standing at the helm,
His particular, personal private realm,
And if you disturb him it's up with your jig;
You'll be clapped in irons and into the brig!"

Aardvark stalked through the cabin door
And dropped his luggage upon the floor—
In black despair on the bunk he sunk,
Dislodging a mink and a skink and a skunk,
Who stuck out their tongues and scurried away
To leave him alone for the rest of the day.
He went to sleep without any supper
On the lower bunk. There was no upper.

Next morn both he and his spirits arose.
"It's because I'm an artist, I suppose.
It's exactly what I might have expected;
Artists have always been neglected.
It's animal nature to be jealous
Of genius in anybody ealous.
If I can't have ants I'll nibble a carrot
And starve in a cabin instead of a garret."
His back grew straighter, his eye grew clearer
As he gazed in his faithful pocket mirror.
"O Aardvark, Aardvark," repeated he,
"How happy I am that I am thee,
And what a glorious world 'twould be
If everybody were just like me!"

With that he donned his beret and smock;
He took his crayons and sketching block;
With a song on his lips and a smile in his heart
He ventured forth to practice his art.

He sat on a stool that was almost dry,
And a passing warthog caught his eye.

"You fortunate creature," he exclaimed,
"Your picture shall be painted and framed.
Into everlasting fame I'll shove you;
I'm going to do a portrait of you."

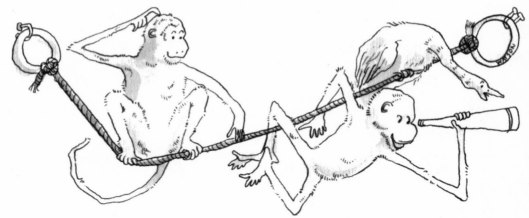

The animals watched while Aardvark sketched;
By now they were sure he was slightly tetched,
And they saw no reason to change their mind
When the masterpiece was finished and signed.
The warthog's inspection at first was curious
But on second glance his complaint was furious.
"You have pictured me with a snorkel snout,
And EX-TEN-SILE tongue a-lolloping out,
And a dangling tail and scooping claws
And mulish ears like twin hee-haws.
That's no warthog I've ever known,
The portrait you've painted is your own."
Was Aardvark astonished? Yes indeed,
But he quickly recovered and spoke his creed.

"Think how much better the world would be
If everybody resembled me.
I thought I was doing a favor to you;
You don't want to look like a warthog, do you?
You don't *really* want to look like you?"
Said the warthog, "Yes I do!"

Aardvark gave a disdainful snort
And moved from starboard across to port
To seek a creature handsome and gallant,
A subject worthy of his talent.
He beheld a tiger and tigress frolicking,
A sight that cured his melancholicking.
While once they might have seemed a menace,
Now they were playing table tennis.

"Tiger," said Aardvark, "while you wait
I'll draw your picture to please your mate."
The tiger simpered and struck a pose
Like Napoleon in stripy clothes,
But, when he saw the portrait finished
His joy was woefully diminished.

"You have pictured me with a snorkel snout
And EX-TEN-SILE tongue a-lolloping out,
And rootless teeth with no enamel
Like those of a TU-BU-LI-DEN-TATE mammal.
That's no tiger I've ever known,
The portrait you've painted is your own!"
Said Aardvark, "But that's the point, you see;
I thought you'd *like* to look like me.
You don't *really* want to look like you?"
Said the tiger, "Yes I do!"

Aardvark kept drawing for seven weeks.
His thanks were grunts and growls and squeaks.
He drew the buffalo and the caribou,
The grizzly bear, the auk, the marabou,
The rhinoceros and the kangaroo,
The kinkajou and the carcajou,
The elephant and the cockatoo,
And creatures never seen in zoo,
But every portrait turned out, alas,
Like Aardvark in his looking glass.
You could hardly hear the rain drops raining
For the noise of animals complaining.

Even the shrew, that tiny elf,
Insisted on looking like himself.
"I may be vicious, I may be small,
But I'm ME, not anyone else at all.
I'd not be you for an emperor's ransom,
No, no, not even if you were handsome."
So Aardvark learned, and not from books,
That each creature liked its very own looks.
And whether from jungles, hills, or veldts,
They didn't want to be anyone else.
They were, though it caused his head to swim,
As proud to be them as he was to be him.

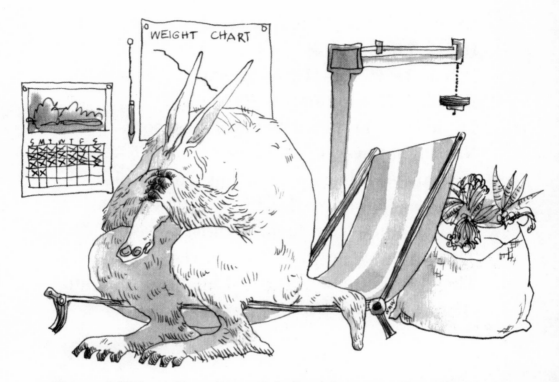

For additional reasons his head was swimming,
His footsteps faltered, his eyes were dimming;
He was more than seven weeks less younger
Than when last an ant had appeased his hunger.
He had barely survived from day to day
On a diet of turnip roots and hay.
A handy deck chair at last he found
And sat down till his head stopped whirling round.

The rain was still wet as a waterspout
When he suddenly heard a stentorian shout:
"Animals, this is your captain speaking;
Put your life-belts on, the ship is leaking;
You must swim like a fish or fly like a gull,
For termites are nibbling a hole in the hull!"

Aardvark uttered a loud "O-ho!"
Recovered his senses and hurried below,
Where he found an army of termites munching,
Gnawing, boring, greedily crunching.
They had chewed a hole in the wooden bottom
Through which you could push a hippopotom.
Like a raging panther Aardvark sprung
He flicked his sticky EX-TEN-SILE tongue,
He sniffed with snout and he scooped with claw
And the termites vanished into his maw.

As soon as his stomach was roundly full
He stuffed the leak with alpaca wool,
And the ship sailed on as light as a feather
Till the forty-first day and shiny weather.

The captain jumped like a young jerboa
And cried, "As sure as my name is Noah
We've reached the point I was aiming at,
We are high and dry on Mount Ararat!"
Then from the animals came a murmur,
"We're pleased to be back on terra firma,
And it's thanks to Aardvark who ate the termites
That we're re-established as terra firmites.

He has saved us all from the rainy blues,
And at last we have had our tropical cruise,
For the sun is out, it's no longer dark,
And he is the Aardvark of the Ark!
O Aardvark, Aardvark, live forever!
You are not only beautiful but clever.
We are happy to look like ourselves, it's true,
But it's lucky for us you look like you.
Oh many a ballad will be sung
Of your glorious sticky EX-TEN-SILE tongue,
Of your scoopy claws and your snorkel snout
That put the wicked termites to rout."
Said Aardvark, "Before adieu I bid you all
I shall portray every individual
Like nobody else, especially me,
But just as he is and wants to be."

He painted the portraits and you can see 'em
If ever you find the right museum.